The Hero
Behind The Sand Dune

Written by:
Susan Houck Blanchard

Illustrated by:
Mackenzie Craig

THE HERO BEHIND THE SAND DUNE

Published by Mindstir Media, LLC
45 Lafayette Rd | Suite 181| North Hampton, NH 03862 | USA
1.800.767.0531 | www.mindstirmedia.com

Printed in the United States of America
ISBN-13: 978-1-7376287-7-4

"Good morning David! We are going to the beach today," said Mom as she entered his bedroom.

David asked, "Can I wear my super hero costume?"

"Not today, we are going to have pictures taken. You need to wear your overalls," explained Mom.

David got dressed, had breakfast and headed to the car with Dad. Dad lifted David up into his car seat and buckled him in.

"So Dad, will I be able to go into the water?" asked David.

Dad responded, "Maybe we can put our feet in the water after pictures are taken."
Then they drove off to the beach. It was a cloudy day, but very warm. When they arrived at the beach, the only person there was the photographer. She took lots of pictures.

After they were done with the pictures, David, Mom and Dad, splashed their feet in the water. It was chilly, but felt nice on their feet.

Then Dad threw David up in the air and caught him.
David felt like he was flying!

David heard some noise and looked up to the sky. He saw a group of seagulls in the sky. The seagulls were yelping loudly!

David pointed and yelled, "Look at the seagulls!"

Then David asked Mom and Dad, "Can I run on the sand to that hill?"

Mom responded, "Yes David, but don't go past the sand dune."

David was very excited! He ran on the white sand. It was as soft as powder. David was hot, but the breeze felt cool.

As David got closer to the sand dune, the seagulls were very loud, circling in the clouds.

Suddenly, a seagull flew down toward David! At first David was scared because the seagull came at him so quickly!

Then surprisingly, the seagull spoke!

"Hi David, I am Sammy Seagull. We need your help! Please come around the sand dune, quickly!"

So David went around, then David screamed, "Oh no! He's stuck!"

There was a little puppy whimpering as it was tangled up in seaweed! The puppy was brown, black and a little white. He was so cute!

David looked at his hands and arms and suddenly felt strong!

David said to Sammy Seagull, "I can help!"

David ran over to the puppy. First he hugged the puppy and then he went to work.

David pulled off some seaweed that was wrapped around the puppy's legs. Then he noticed one leg was cut, just above the paw. That piece of seaweed was hard to break. David pulled with both hands to rip it apart. He used all his muscle and strength! Then the puppy was free!

Sammy Seagull shouted with joy, "David, you saved him!"

David felt so happy! He picked up the puppy, holding him in his arms, and said softly, "You're going to be OK now."

The sky had gotten very dark with clouds.

David said, "Sammy Seagull, I need to get back to my Mom and Dad."

Sammy flew up high to the sky and came back down.

Sammy pointed straight ahead and told David, "They are right over there!"

David replied, "Thank you Sammy Seagull."

Sammy Seagull said, "Thank you David for all your help! You were so kind to help us! You are very strong too!"

David carried the puppy and began running to his Mom and Dad. He gave the puppy to Dad. Mom picked up David, giving him a big hug.

Dad asked, "David, where did you find this puppy?"

David explained, "He was stuck behind the sand dune. He was trapped in seaweed and crying. I pulled apart the seaweed to set him free."

Mom said as she smiled, "You are his hero David!" Then Mom said, "I will bandage his leg when we get home. We need to leave now, a storm is coming."

So they all headed home with David's new friend. They gave the puppy a bath and Mom wrapped the puppy's leg with bandage.

David went to bed with the puppy next to him.

David was hugging his new cuddly friend and said, "I will call you Sam, so that we don't forget our friend, Sammy Seagull." Then David said softly, "I love you Sam."

David saw his super hero costume in the corner of his room and thought, I can be a super hero without a costume. Then David smiled and went to sleep.

CPSIA information can be obtained
at www.ICGtesting.com
Printed in the USA
BVHW020741090921
615761BV00002B/4